PRINT EDITION

STORMDANCER© 2015 Mirror World Publishing and Joshua Pantalleresco
Illustrations and cover art © 2015 Florence Chan
Edited by Kristen Denbow and Justine Alley Dowsett
All Rights Reserved. Published by Mirror World Publishing October 1st, 2015

Mirror World Publishing
Windsor, Ontario
www.mirrorworldpublishing.com
info@mirrorworldpublishing.com
Mirror World Publishing publications data available upon request

ISBN: 978-0-9947490-3-1

STORMDANCER

Written by

Joshua Pantalleresco

Illustrated by

Florence Chan

Edited by

Kristen Denbow

No Journey is Walked Alone

I wanted to take a moment, before I thank everyone that contributed to this book, to thank each and every person that I've managed to work with the last five years at my day job. Specifically, I have a big list of people that I've managed to come across and want to thank for their part in my journey. So thanks to: Dave Liggins, Jeff Thomson, Dean Berry, "Mr. DJ" Bob Proctor, Benny Williams, Ryan Stoddart, Jordan Shanahan, Nena S. Lumen, Ghalia Farage (I don't care!), Brian Ekwulugo, Kathy Ordinaria, Patrick Schmith, Robin Fowldes, Ron Ramey, Tim Lane, Nathan Barteaux, Jodie Lintelow, Jerrad Orser, Abdulgani Bihi, Brandon McLean, and his dad Richard, for the many rides home. I also want to take a moment to mention some former employees as well. Sarah Valcourt, Balkan Farage, Gordon Langley, Megan Buckboro, Jeremy Luzzi, and Maxwell Fritsch. Finally, I want to give a special thank you to Jason Benjamin, who went to bat for me when he didn't have to. This is a small token of my appreciation, bud. May you find what's out there. You all have been fun, amazing people and I want to thank each and every one of you. To those I missed mentioning; sorry. It's on me.

Now to the book: I want to thank my collaborators Florence Chan and Kristen Denbow. You guys made me better and this book wouldn't have been the same without you.

I want to thank my publishers, Justine Ally Dowsett and Murandy Damodred for publishing my work and believing in me. I want to also mention Justine's husband Robert, who goes out of his way to share my random facebook and twitter posts the world over. Thank you.

Lance Buan and James Julin are secretly two of the coolest people ever. Lance is my favorite dude to jam with, and James is secretly a good – maybe great – man. They go out of their way to help me and I am thankful. These words are small. Also, their significant others, Alicen Buan and Caliegh Cassidy. Caliegh, I always appreciate your willingness to punch me on cue, and Ally, thank you for being able to put up with me.

I want to thank some professionals that have made me better people. Dirk Manning for showing me what it takes to be rock star. You pave the way for many, my friend. Brian Hades, I want to thank for his occasional gentle nudging here and there to keep me on the path I chose. I want to take this moment to thank Simon Rose for making me step up my game with interviews. I owe you huge for how I grew there.

To my friends JR Stewart and Cory McConnachie for surviving living with me. For my friends Shelniel Bostic and Raymond McClellan for being kind enough to put up with me at the moment. Lastly, for Randall Unland and Justin McClellan for having the same angel like patience that Shelniel and Raymond have.

I thank my Dad, always. He's in my corner and bets on me. He always has. Love you.

My Nanna, for being my Nanna. She raised me and made me strong. I love you.

Lastly, to the Almighty. Thank you for being there for me. I love you, too.

To My Sister

I believe in you, and I always have

I. Ruined Pasts

this isn't just my story anymore

walking back to my own, I grow nervous

will they like the world I created?

will it be enough where the river ends?

possibilities swirl

as well as my panic

and wonder

where do we go from here?

what do we want to do?

For now, I want to take them home

show them my little space

teach them the concept of 'mine'

transform it into 'theirs'

Wild Will looks at the oozes roaming around

grabbing a carrot to dangle in front of them

should I warn him about the bigger ones?

Nicki is frightened

a mouse in a sea of cats

the world is ferocious even without dragons

I remember my first time out

unsure if I belonged

I still don't know the answer

I do know I can do this

Kristen is the one that worries me

she hasn't said a word all night

sometimes I think I nearly see tears fall from her face

the rest of the time, her expression is stone

should I say something?

do nothing?

I don't know

talking to others about their problems

isn't something I do

we all walk through the forest and follow the river

past the grounded chariot

which still sits there silent and lifeless

watching us pass it by

we watch the river stretch out and expand

soon we will be home

a strange feeling

I never felt this way about the compound and the tower

at times, I miss the view

the one nice thing about being the Watcher

had been the endless expanse of the horizon

the world seemed endless from above

where the river ends is a compromise

my view isn't as far up from the ground

but the water itself goes over the edge of the world

there is an endless sunset

into a distant dawn

every day

only there is no abyss gazing back

I feel at peace with that view

something I never felt back where I was born

it was mine

No.

Theirs

Ours

it is great to not be alone

to know that at long last we will be safe

my meager stick of a home can now grow

become a small hearth where we share stories

dreaming dreams without dragons...

all is ruined at river's end.

my home already reduced to ash

the sand around it changed to glass

all that was mine is no more

I grip my ebony blades in rage

who would dare do this to me?

didn't they know that this was mine?

my blood boils

I want to make them pay

II. The Hunted

I examine the sword

curved and round like the moon

it is entrenched in my ruined hearth

no power can help me lift it from the earth

it stands there

defiant

overpowering

the message is clear

a red haze beckons

I understand and nearly roar

I know you, I mutter to myself

I understand what you're saying

you're bigger than me

stronger

you know where I live

and you can do this to me

I don't fear you

you think you are out there hunting me

but it's I who am hunting you

I look at my friends

and suddenly feel lost

what do I do with them?

this isn't just my story anymore

there is so much they have not seen

or done

will they be safe without me?

will I really feel better seeking revenge?

I don't know

I am angry and scared

savage and violent

without a clue what to do next

I look at my blackened blades

forever stained with the blood of dragons

they gleam

it had been a while since they feasted

tonight

they would do so again

so I run

I follow the trail back into the forest

the footprints beacons and crumbs for me to pursue

listening to the sounds of the forest

I hear the eternal struggles of my friends, the rabbits and the

ooze

the werecat in the distance

wary

he isn't here, whoever he is

but I am patient and cunning

I can wait

I listen to the music of the forest

crouching in the bushes and trees

I blend in

waiting for him to appear

eventually the music dies

silence is all that remains

he is out there

all I have to do is grasp my blade and then...

out of the corner of my eye

I see him

a large dragon

tall and wiry

his wings in chains

moving without a sound

he sniffs the air

looking in my direction

a cunning, faraway look in his eyes

does he know I'm here?

does he see me?

before I can lunge

he pauses, unsure

I wait

eternity passes

he decides to walk away

silently, slowly

he takes a step back

I take the bait

about to move forward when...

what am I doing?

why am I here?

my anger and fear

took on a life of its own

boiling over inside

becoming a quiet storm

my life is a mess

everyone is gone

mom, dad,

everybody back home

all gone

forever

I thought dying would be a journey

but it is the absolute end

I feel like I am forsaken

I never thought I'd feel so alone

I left them all behind

Kristen, frozen, silent

as broken as I am

Wild Will

curious, contrary

unsure of what his nature holds

Nicki,

scared and fragile

trembling at the world I've thrust upon her

what have I done?

I am so caught up

listening only to the turmoil

that I ignore the silence of the forest

until I feel an arm constrict my throat

before I can blink

a swipe disarms me

and the arm squeezes

it becomes hard to breathe

I struggle

biting, scratching

clawing, kicking

his other arm coils behind my head

my neck feels like it is being crushed

before the forest starts to dim

I feel sleepy

after a while

I forget all about the struggle

all about the storm

and I close my eyes

drifting off to sleep

falling into a cage of darkness

III. Storms Within

he ran

disappearing into the night

leaving us all alone

we tried to follow *him*

but were unsure of the trees and trails

we went slowly

we knew something had happened

when we found *his* blades in the forest

blackened and alone

he had come

like a force of nature

wrecking our lives

in the name of freedom

freedom from what?

the hollow embers and ashes we found

I didn't build them

those ruins were *his* story

not mine

never mine

I...was happy

yeah, I was happy

is there something wrong with that?

my parents loved me

I didn't care about anything else

the dragons were bastards

but I understood the game

the moves that could be made

with one flick of a blade

he changed all that

shattered the illusion with a roar of rebellion

now my life is here

in this forest

now *he* had vanished into the night

leaving me abandoned

leaving everything in shambles!

Mom...Dad...

I tried to cry for you

tried to mourn when they mourned

doing what everyone else is doing

just like always

no tears have managed to fall

I stand out for the first time

I hate this

I hate this more than anything

for the first time in my life

I don't know what to do

I am just numb

I feel absolutely nothing

I wish I could feel this way forever

but life moves on

regardless of how I feel

my parents are still dead

he has still disappeared

Will and Nicki look on

worrying about *him*

wondering where *he* went

and if they can follow

they seem okay about all that has happened

they cried those first few nights

but *he* reassured them

cried with them

let out their pain

I couldn't

is there something wrong with me?

they think *he* is missing

another footprint is found

large and dragon-like

forcing its impression on the forest

there had been a struggle

I know fear

what had happened to *him*?

do I really want to find out?

what to do?

they want to find *him*

I realize that I do too

why, I have no clue

but I need to sort all this out

a gaping dragon-shaped hole is in front of us

footprints lead in the opposite direction

he hadn't gone quietly

whoever had taken *him* was already moving

we had to catch them and fast

I look to the others and nod

we start after *him*

we are going to find *him*

no matter what

IV. Into the Unknown

we follow the broken trail
fumbling through the forest and trees
still learning how to move
this isn't like the compound
this trail was carved with *his* blades

who is the hunter
and why did they only capture *him*?
why not capture us all, if they bested *him*?

is this a trap?

it would makes sense if it was

maybe they could only take one of us

or maybe they thought there was just *him*

all we know is that we must press forward

Nicki, the mouse

Wild Will

and Me, the girl of stone

Nicki seems unsure of the forest

it makes her feel smaller than she already feels

a mouse moving in a giant field

wondering if large predators watch her

Will...

I can't even begin to know what he is thinking

he acquired (stole) the lens *he* has

the one that makes distances seem smaller

and is using it to examine the ground

he had been using it at the camp before

looking at all the little things around us

grabbing and bugs and things that seem gross

that's what I saw anyway

he sees a world

other people slaving in tinier places

building their own kingdoms beneath us

he wonders if they have dragons too

I think he's crazy

worlds within worlds...

does that mean there is something bigger out there?

something larger building vaster worlds than this?

do they even know we're here?

I shake my head

there can't be more...can there?

Will examines the battle between the dragon and *him*

trying to puzzle out what happened

where they are heading

he finds something

and picks it up

shows it to Nicki and I

it is a scale

one like I've seen on many a dragon

taking me back to the time of the pits

my parents telling me stories in front of the fire...

I brush those memories aside

not quite letting them go

watching Will point in a direction

that-a-way then

that's where the dragon went

none of us have been that way

not even *him*

this would be a different journey

part of me wants to stop right here

is it wrong to be afraid?

I don't like this forest

or those ruined ashes of the thing called 'home'

this place is alien to me

what lies ahead will be worse

this, at least, was *his*

there is a comfort in that

would I be able to let *him* go?

would I be able to forgive myself if I did?

no

we have to journey into the unknown

we have to see where this all leads

what awaits us on the other side

I nod

let us go then

see what is out there

even if all I want is to go home

V. New Horizons

our trek is slow

we hear screams and growls

the hissing motion of oozes

the crunch of teeth biting down on flesh

the forest itself snarls against us leaving

we follow the broken trail of footprints

human and dragon alike

hindered by our own uncertainty

are we getting closer?

or are they growing farther apart?

we refuse to think we're losing them

we have to keep going

the trail is clear

like breadcrumbs mapping out our route

daring us to follow

we'll get closer one step at a time

in time, the forest stops snarling

its struggles grow feeble

as we hunt and trap

we learn the art of patience

and reward ourselves with what the forest can provide

the first kill is difficult

we catch a rabbit in a snare

it lies there, motionless

waiting for the end to come

I hold the knife to its throat

his knife

seeing the fear in its face

as I go to strike down

I can't

I just can't

it looks at me

pleading its case

forcing me to show it mercy

Nicki grabs the knife from my hands

plunges it into its heart

the rabbit's pleas become lifeless

there is innocence lost

we are both shaken by what she did

our stomachs growl and quell our disdain

she looks down at the rabbit with relish

and so do I

this empty shell is not a rabbit anymore

just meat

and we are hungry

more time passes

the forest transforms into flocks of trees

open space peeking its way into our world

each of us has learned to kill

slaves to our hunger

but we have learned how to survive

doing what we have to

we have become hunters

and now I understand *him*

he had talked about *his* battles with the deer

and I thought *him* foolish

we have not slain anything quite so large

but we have learned to eat and forage

there is honesty in that

I can see now how *he* enjoyed it

the space that poked its head expands

becoming fields of grain and gold

corn and wheat and weeds sparkle everywhere

the occasional hill breaking the sameness of it all

for a second, I am reminded of the fields we toiled in

but for all our work

we couldn't match this wild patch

this, I realize, is how it should be

the trail becomes harder to find in the open plains

no broken limbs or trees to act as guideposts

our compass is broken

we are unsure how to proceed

unnatural calm and fear grips us

have we lost them somehow?

silence

then, a scream

the wind rushes by behind me

it is my only warning

if I hadn't stumbled

I'd have felt piercing claws rake my back

instead I tumble down, hearing a shriek of rage

it is both bird and dragon

eagle claws and raven beak

with long reptilian dragon wings

black mane and feathers

dark as the night

and more terrifying

it looks at me with predator eyes

all three of us freeze in fear

hypnotized by our impending deaths

its second shriek mobilizes us

adrenaline washes over me

I feel my heart beating

my blood rushing

and my feet move with a life of their own

we dash into the taller corn field where it might not find us

how are we going to survive?

his knife is not my weapon

it is a toothpick compared to those claws

which might as well be swords

yet we have to do something

we could run

scatter

it would not catch us all

but in our fear we might lose each other

I couldn't bear that

I can't lose any more of them!

we've come too far

to lose each other now

I will not allow this thing to take any more of us

there has to be something we can do!

the bird eyes us all

soaring above us in a circle

it is scanning us

searching for weakness

I look through the corn

looking for something

anything

to help us

I grip something hollow

it doesn't feel like the wheat in the field

rather something man-made

it feels thick and useful

I pull at it

and pull at it

until I feel the ground give it to me

I hear its cries behind me

I do not hesitate

I swing the hollow thing

connecting the tip of it to its head

flesh and bone break on impact

and my arms are numbed by the collision

the giant writhes in pain

fear grips its predator's heart

it changes its mind about us

and flees

seeking easier meat

today, it would not be us

I look at the mighty stick in my hand

a treasure from the lost age?

it is white and smooth

with long and hollow ends

inscribed in a language I've never seen

it had been abandoned here, long ago

I look at *his* blades

and realize that they aren't for me

they cut and slash and claw at enemies

they are jagged and vicious

something I want no part of

the staff is solid

hollow

it has no edges

it is just a strapping strong reed that won't give

this is Me

and these are *him*

and while *he* is different from Me

I realize I love *him* all the same

I vow to give these back to *him*

I will find *him* no matter what

I look at the others

they are safe

and it makes me smile

maybe I'm not quite so hollow inside

we press on

seeking the trail we had spotted so easily before

the pursuit isn't over

VI. Slings and Stones

as we travel, the plains expand

long hills, gleaming green and silver, paint the canvas of the

world around us

bamboo becomes cactus

and the trees are now spiked and sharp

thorny and insurmountable

I glance at the fruit at the top of a tree

hunger gnawing at me

on instinct, I reach for the trunk

stopping just before its needles prick me

vexed, I glance up

there has to be a way to get to it

but how?

Will and Nicki notice my plight

the same pangs of hunger surging in them

we can't climb the tree

my stick, as long as it is

barely stretches along the surface

the fruit hovers in the air

untouchable

I look around

there has to be something

anything

to grab the prize

all we have are sticks and stones

some shaped like X's and Y's

unnatural shapes in the wild

Will examines the sticks and stones

finding a large Y-shaped stick

rough and unrefined

we watch the gears in his head work

as an answer comes to him

Will grabs *his* knife

and uses it to chip away at the Y-shaped wood

cutting away the excess

refining its shape

I almost tell him to stop

when I realize he is building something

shaping

rearranging

creating

destroying

until he is satisfied with what is in his hands

once satisfied, he looks around

finding some clustered weeds and vines

he ties them together, making crude fibers

until it all comes together

elastic and taut at the same time

it is crude, but it is finished

and we are proud

Will grabs a rock on the ground

puts in in the middle of the tied up vines

stretching them out by pulling it away from the Y-shaped stick

aiming and firing at the fruit

the rock zips

I hear it hit the tree with a thunk

missing the fruit at the top

Nicki grabs the tool Will made

and uses her eye to take careful aim

roaring loudly

Nicki fires

determined to get the prize

the stone fires

the thunk is different

silent

compared to the thomp of the trunk

the fruit falls

tumbling to the ground

we roar in victory

our hunger would be satisfied

we had done it

together

VII. City of Dragons

we fed and gorged ourselves
licking our lips after the sweet prize from above
once finished, we resume our chase
who knows how far they are now?

there is still no sign of *him*
the trail has become jagged
twisted

we wonder to ourselves

after all this time

have we lost our way?

the sky and air darken

no dragon-birds storm the skies

there is only the odd screech of an eagle

as giant serpents slither below

their tongues and scales neon indigo

a few lizard-cats still roam

bigger and fatter than the ones we left behind

lazy and content to just lay there

watching us pass them by

we press forward

unsure if we are right

our destination a mystery

the darkness grows

casting shadows on the land

darkened holes scorch the ground around us

scars from long ago

a tower stands on the horizon
tall and defiant to the passage of time

little squares can be made out in the distance
is this another compound of dragons?
do people dream of freedom here?
or, like us, never thought of it
until they too had a Watcher in their midst?

I can't help but smile at that hope
something is changing in me
I am starting to think a little like *him*
to understand a little of *his* freedom

how to approach?
do we go around it, or through?

I ask the others
and Nicki surprises me with her answer
she wants to press on

I look at her
she too, has changed
no longer the mouse

skittering here and there

sticks and stones have made her strong
she strides now with every step
a giant in the land

Will echoes her sentiment
he seems more comfortable in the wild
letting his fists do the talking
while his mind expands

and me?
I want to go and see as well
I have never seen a city
when would I get this chance again?

it takes longer than it should
we are cautious
we have grown used to freedom
we don't want to lose it to a dragon patrol

the squares in the distance
become houses up close
we see movement in them

we move more cautiously

there are no fortifications
the buildings are from the old days
when things like concrete and steel were commonplace
they stand tall and proud
yet time has still taken its toll
chips pool around the foundations
litter decorates each house
salves to wounds of decay

there is so much noise
chatter comes from endless places
microphones blare out recordings that are musical
playing their pleasant sounds again and again
it is hard to think after all the silence

food smells permeate the air
I smell cherries and something else, sweet and delicious
fouled only by the scent of garbage and sewage
smoky flavours
remind me a little of home
but something alien as well
this place seems...larger somehow

humans walk the streets

with dragons alongside them

no guns or swords or whips or chains among them

all seems peaceful and harmonious

there is an order to things

we look around

incredulous

is this real?

VIII. Strangers

it is all so big and new
strange to see dragons and men walking side by side
even stranger to feel the butterflies in my stomach

is there something amiss?
no, there can't be
there is no hostility
tensions don't exist here

or do they?

I look around

it isn't side by side

dragons walk ahead

there is dominance there

an order to things

I understand it all too well

maybe we are wrong

maybe it is different

but slavery is still slavery

chains are still chains

no matter what form they take

the humans are not dressed as we were in our compound

their clothes are more sophisticated

layered

black coats and white shirts

with a little flutter in the middle

the women wear dresses and something ornate around their

necks

at first I think it is a collar

but then I see what it really is

it seems like it is both armor and for show

a game I don't really understand

I decide I prefer my simple clothes

I start to dislike this city of dragons

the humans talk

but the language is harsh

they seem to have friendly faces

but I see anger in their eyes when they look at each other

they aren't talking

they are competing

fighting for the favour of the dragons in front of them

or maybe the little stones the dragons use to trade?

what is it called?

cur-en-cy?

it seems so alien

yet so familiar

I look up and ask the Wandering God

do we ever build anything different on our own?

can we only build prisons for ourselves?

is slavery all we have to offer?

have we always been this small?

or am I imagining what I see here?

I am just a stranger here

I feel eyes look down on us

seeing us for the first time

we look back at the dragons looking down on us

recognizing the looks we had gotten in our own compound

those eyes are terrifying

all consuming

devouring

they can never be satisfied

they only want

one of the dragons reaches down

with its scaly hands

those same eyes never wavering

we know that look all too well

I saw it every day when I worked in the fields

those same hungry eyes watched us

seeing us as property

while we worked for their harvest

I remember *him* coming back and bringing fire

I understand *him* now, perfectly

Nicki strikes first

a stone finds its mark on the crown of the dragon's head

surprised looks come from the onlookers' faces

seeing black blood oozing to the ground

we move quickly

Will charges first

tackling the stunned dragon

to the sharp gasps of the human pets behind it

the dragon hisses in pain

as its body crashes hard into the ground

Will lands on top of it, hammering down with his fists

I rush the other

swinging my stick

it connects right with its snout

I hear a hiss of fear and surprise

and follow through with a thrust to its chest

I feel a bone break

and blood trickles down its mouth

burning the ground below

suddenly we are surrounded

dragons and humans circle us

I feel surprise and betrayal at the human cattle with them

despair threatens me

was I, too, like this when this all started?

what a fool I had been

but how can we win here?

there is no backup

no parents

no army

he isn't here either

is this how it is going to end?

No!

I growl

Not like this!

If I am going to go down

I am going to rage at every inch I have to give

they are not going to have me surrender

they will have to earn their victory

I swing my staff

Will, his fists

Nicki, her stones

and for a time

we hold

until they grab us

I hear my stick clatter to the ground

a human fist aims for my face...

and everything goes black

IX. Jailbreak

I awake to metal bars around me
I'm lying in a perfect square
other prisoners stand around me
I am a prisoner again
this time the cage is literal

I am furious
how long have we been here?

how much time have we lost?

The trail has to have gone cold by now

tears trickle down my face

before I furiously choke them back

no

I'm not going to cry here

not now!

I'm not going to give up

we have come so far

we can't stop now

in this cell

I face myself

and move past the void in my heart

all the anger and hate and rage at all I've lost comes loose

all my pain

my rage

all I've lost is here

I can't run or hide from it anymore

it, like me, is locked in a cage

I am tired of this cell I carried

I can't do it anymore

I let go

letting out my rage

my loss

letting all the love I hold for my friends

and family take its place

I have grown on this journey

I am not the girl that started

and this isn't just about finding *him*

I have my own story to tell

my own family to protect

I'm not going to leave any of them behind

I examine the cell I'm in and the ones around it

there is a hall between the cells

and in it a man is reading something

relaxed by the bars that hold us here

unconcerned by the hostile glares directed at him

Will is in another cell

surrounded by other prisoners

all of them human

each looking at the other with mistrust

Nicki looks defiant in her cell

her eyes are cold and angry

even the biggest, strongest looking men and women

are quelled by the gaze of my friend

I have no idea why the other prisoners are being held

some have the same eyes as the dragons

predatory and all-devouring

others are scared

just like us

we have to get out of here

I whistle

Will and Nicki look at me

both with relief

I am touched by their concern

the guard looks at the three of us

then gazes back down at his scroll

we are just children, he seems to think

what could we do?

I howl

Will and Nicki join me

the other prisoners follow suit

our screams join in unison

the common desire to be free roars in us all

the guard puts down his scroll and stands

he bangs on our cells

speaking with command in his voice

we ignore him

screaming to the heavens

the building bristles at our screams

shaking in protest at the sound of our voices

the walls shed their skin

pieces falling to the ground

the guard motions for someone down the hall

two men with visors and shades dressed all in black trudge down

they come to my cell and point at me

their demands for silence made apparent by the clanking of their

sticks

so like mine

I keep screaming

defiant to the end

I am not afraid of their sticks

nor of the promise of pain

I've already been down this road before

and...

opportunity presents itself

they still think me a child

when the key turns

and the door opens

two guards walk in and try to smother me

hold me down so the third can put me down

I evade the first

and slide under the second

lunging at the third

the one holding the keys

I punch him in the throat

surprised, he drops to his knees

dropping the keys to the ground

I go after them

I don't have much time

I grab them and head for the cell door
fumbling with the keys
I search for the one that clicks with the lock
before tumbling to my knees in agony
as I feel a painful thwack of a stick right to my back
the guards won't let me escape so easily

I can't breathe, much less move
so close and yet so far
I feel hands wrap around my throat
I feel the room grow dim

I can't stop now
but what can I do?

the key!
where's the key?
one second it was in the cell door
the next, it has vanished
where can it have gone?

my vision dims

and I almost fade into oblivion

before all goes black

the hands around my throat are suddenly gone

I collapse to the floor

looking up at the pandemonium

a few prisoners hold the guards I'd evaded down

taking turns exacting retribution

I see the key in the cell door

freedom a mere turn away

I crawl and hurry

knowing we don't have much time

more guards come down the hall

men and dragons both

I turn the key with all my might

opening the door

tumbling back to the ground

watching the open door make caged animals men again

charging at the men and dragons that jailed them

each trying to stop the other

I remember our compound on fire

and know this too will end in flame

is this all we know?

can we not do better than this?

I feel arms grab me

I stand up, shaky

Will and Nicki are beside me

free of their own cells

looking for a way out

we need to leave

this city didn't welcome us

there has to be something better out there

something more than a city of dragons

we crawl

slide down the hall

and find a sewer gate, just like the one we had back home

only to open it and find it to be much much worse

how do these people manage to live here?

We hear sounds of men shouting

screaming and hissing, angry shouts

they are looking for us

we have to hurry

we plug our noses

and jump in

hoping that no one will follow us

as we vanish into the darkness

we have escaped

but into what?

the question haunts us in the darkness

where do we go from here?

X. Echoes of Stars

we trudge through...I don't even want to think about it

it is slimy and clingy and stinky

I hold my breath as long as I can

letting myself breathe only when I have to

I can't imagine how the others are handling it

eventually, I slip

sliding down the rapid waters

swept up for the ride

I try to struggle against the current
but only go under for my troubles
I gasp and cough
do my best to relax so I float
I have no idea where the sewer leads

I see gleaming white light in the distance
before being spat out of the city
and into a pond

all of us come up for air
our eyes darting around
looking for a chance to get away from the sludge

the edge isn't far
we let the running water push us toward the shore
pulling up onto the ledge one by one
feeling dirty and relieved at the same time

we look up to the city
seeing, not the wonder and alienness of it
but the hollowness

the rot within

once men lived here in freedom

now dragons walk among them

and nothing is the same

all this bluster

trying to forget

that we failed

there is no trail to follow anymore

he is gone

I can't believe it

don't want to believe

that we'll never see *him* again

that time we had spent caged up

then washing up here, who knows where

there is no way *he* could have come this way

we are just here

caught in a storm

going to and fro like rain

with no control over where and how we fall

only that there is a bottom

there is no way we are still on *his* path

just thinking about it makes me want to...

no!

I won't!

I'm not going to cry here!

there has to be some way to find *him*

but I don't know how

none of us do!

I have failed

what else is there to say?

we look up to the stars

even though less shine here in the shadow of the city

a few specks sparkle in the night

there isn't a full shape in the sky

but a few dare to look down on us

back in the compound, I had asked Mom and Dad where the

stars came from

that night, at storytime, they told me

all of us

about the origin of the stars

during a great cataclysm
the Wandering God searched for a place of safety
somewhere to gather as many people as he could

he found the sky above him
and he darted off
taking the ones he could save with him
until they were safe
shining lights in the darkness

they are still out there
wandering
waiting for the rest of us to come home

I used to gaze up before bedtime
wondering exactly where they were
and if I could join them

going through the city
I realized that there is some truth to it
there are other places out there
things I've never seen
wonders just waiting to be discovered

I just have to go out and find them

that night we sleep in turns
I watch my new family slumber
as I reflect on the disasters of today

like *he* had, I have become something else
I howled at men and dragons alike
rebelled at the order of things
told them I am not a beast to be caged
I am free

I had faced down dragons in the wilderness
and now in this foul place

the echoes of stars flicker out
looking up, I pray to the Wandering God
like when I was a child
I long for the stars
one day, I hope to be up there
soaring in a place without dragons

for a while, I am content

XI. Choices

we press on

what else is there to do?

I hope against hope that we'll find the trail again

as I dread the unsaid truth among us

the stink from last night still lingers

the mountains of metal we trudge through don't help

we thought the city was disgusting

but these giant holes in the ground are like cities of garbage

my feet crunch against metal and glass

smells of garbage and other ancient things surround us

it is like the city, but isn't

Will grabs something clear and slick

we all touch its surface

it is oily and slick

and crinkles on contact

an old material

I've seen nothing like it

something the ancients used?

It is small and the top opens

something to carry small things?

a bag?

Nicki holds another small thing with a silly dog face on the top

it is small, handheld and very narrow

pulling on the dog's head

causes an empty neck to pop out

we all freak out and run

what kind of weirdos were we back then?

Will spots it first

another grounded chariot

sitting on top of one of the mounds of metal

symbols dancing along its surface

moving around with different patterns and colours

are they letters?

words?

I have no idea

this is the second craft we've seen

had the dragons come from the stars themselves?

or had we?

we press on

seeking to leave this ancient place behind

like the city, it is a tomb

one I can't wait to leave

we walk forever

until trees clash with metal

and win the battle at last

the sky brightens

and a stream forms at the start of a forest

we follow the water

little bits of garbage clutter with the fish

creating a layer of grey sludge at the bottom

walking along the stream

the skies turn grey and darken once again

it isn't the eternal night of the city

but the darkness of a storm

thunder sounds and lightning shoots upward in the distance

this is like no storm I've ever seen

wave upon wave of lightning shoots up from the ground

thunder echoes on the horizon

as we approach the edge of the storm

we see the bones of men and beasts decorating the landscape

many have tried to cross this

only to burn

we stop at the edge of the storm

can we go any further?

should we turn back?

I have no idea where *he* is

only that the city is back there

and we don't want to go to that hateful place again

what do I do?

I don't know

and worse yet

they look at me

like I have all the answers

do my friends share my doubts?

what can I say to them?

give up, after all we've been through?

I don't know what to do

how do you go forward?

when you have no idea what is coming?

when there are no guarantees left at all?

Is it so wrong to have doubts?

no matter what I want

the world keeps moving

it cares not one whit about any illusions I have

only that it will still be here tomorrow

dragging me every inch along with it

thunder rumbles

my hopes are dashed with the roar

the bones are still in the distance

going forward or back

I would be destroyed either way

I hate the thought

I like who I am right now

only it isn't enough

this world will take

and keep taking

until I am no more

I could go back into the city

find a way to swallow my pride

live among dragons once again

and betray everything I've done to get this far

take the family I have left

and exist

or I can journey into the storm

hope against hope that I will see *him* again

and find a new home somewhere out there

maybe even among the stars

or never find anything at all

I have to let go of something

it is up to me

they look to me

I can't stop doubting

wondering if I am doing the right thing

but I have to finish this

I have to keep moving forward no matter what

freezing cold and tired

I realize that I want this

I need to see where this goes

I've come this far

I might as well go a little further

even if it kills me

I look up at the lightning

and where I stand

I am a step away from the storm

amazing, what a difference one step can make

just when I am about to take the plunge, I hear a voice

turning around

I see a man dressed all in white

he raises his hands slowly

non-threateningly

gesturing for us to come closer

we look at him, but don't see anything in his face but concern

he reminds me of some of the others we had grown up with

he gestures us closer and points

there is a tower on the horizon

white as the coat he is wearing

a beam of light shines in the distance

and I realize we are being offered shelter from the storm

I take it

and we follow him to his home

XII. Languages

the tower is one of the old buildings
tall and defiant to the passage of time
it seems made of tinted glass
the ruins around it are desolate
whatever else stood here is long gone

inside the place is hollow
it feels cut away from the the world outside

the halls are silent, unchanging

it has the feeling of a tomb

the man in white guides us down stairs

to a door marked with red and yellow

he takes a small square card and inserts it into the wall

a red light turns on

we hear a bell

and the door opens to another room

other men and women in white are on the other side

each watching a moving image

it is hypnotic

the lightning moves

over and over again

how is it possible?

amused, the man heads to a machine

and pushes a button

we all blink as

the image disappears

Will wanders to the machine
the man nods
he presses the switch again
the lightning comes back on the screen
flashing over and over

magic from our past
this must be the ancients' work

Will cackles with glee and starts pressing the button on and off
Nicki shakes her head
cuffing Will behind the ear
to make him stop

ancient symbols appear on the screen
writing themselves in the lightning
numbers and letters seemed to be being made by each flash
from the earth
is this a message of some kind?

Will studies it
interested
he spies a pattern
and watches a symbol repeat over and over again

hot beverages are put in our hands

the strangers look at us

and we at them

they aren't like the others

no dragons are in their midst

they seem to be doing their own thing

studying the lightning

if such a thing is possible

our guide approaches us

waving something in his hands

pointing it at himself and then repeating it

after a few times, I put it together

this is his name

he points at all of us

gesturing for us to sound out our names

I go first

I say it out loud, nice and slow

"Krist-in"

he gestures for me to repeat it

his face both eager and trusting

when I do so, he conjures up another symbol

giving it to me

he sounds out his name "Jord-an"

and does that symbol I first saw him perform

then says my name "Krist-in"

making the symbol he had manifested

he points to the drinks we have in our hands

enunciating the phrase "coff-ee" and revealing another symbol

nodding, we take sips from our offered drinks

the drink is bitter

yet strong

I am suddenly more awake

more aware of the world around me

communication is slow

but through the symbols Jordan makes

we manage to have a dialogue with his family

they are using the image before them to study the lightning

the storm without end

there are these little flecks of silver and grey dust in the storm

they are small and invisible

only magic, like the screen from the past, can see them

somehow, these flecks had created the storm

keeping the lightning going forever and ever

we watch the image magnify

like the lens Will carries

we see the little gleams of silver and grey

they seem to talk and say the same thing

dot dot dot

line line line

dot dot

line

Will says it aloud

sure enough, it is another gesture

another language to be learned

we just have to find out what it is saying

XIII. Calling

dot dot dot

line line line

every day

it is a pattern

the scientists compile their data

hoping to understand

what are the little cells of grey and silver saying?

how do we communicate back to them to figure it out?

dot dot dot

tap tap?

Nicki taps

for each dot on the line she taps

dot dot dot

tap tap tap

line line

twirl?

could it really be that simple?

the men and women in white stop to watch

dot dot

tap tap

we all try to fumble our way through

it clicks somehow

the dots and lines are patterns

our movements, clumsy and fumbling

fit a pattern of their own

a language of our own making

my first time is scary

doing the steps

the taps

the twirls

makes me feel awkward

but once I ignore the people around

focus on the dots

concentrate on the steps

there is a beat

moving with the message

of lightning and thunder without rain

it feels invigorating

this storm-dancing

it all becomes a blur

I add my own slant to the rhythm

spinning into a full pirouette

adding pivots to the steps

I feel alive in a way I've never felt before

I am discovering something new within myself

I want to keep doing this

not just to try and talk to the storm

but for me

I could do this forever

I stop after the image fades

the dots and lines long gone

I face the stares of my audience

and all of them clap

I think of *him* with each clap

he had been right all along

there is more to this world than the compound

there is dancing

thunder roars in the distance

lightning fizzles from the ground

there is only one thing left to do...

XIV. Stormdancer

lightning flashes without end

occasional streaks of silver flash within it

thunder booms all around

dot dot dot

line line line

remains of animals lie in front of me

an audience waiting for this performance

I am scared

I think to myself how silly this all is

trying to talk to lightning with a dance

seems so absurd to me

but I have to try

I want to be free

I want to go beyond the storm

I smile a sad smile

before we begin

I understand *him* now completely

he saw a door and wanted to open it

this is no different

it booms, it crackles

it thunders, it sears

but in the end, this storm too, is a door

I only have to walk through it

I miss my staff

the desire to twirl it grabs me

I can hear my heart beating rapidly

I close my eyes

and breathe

I wear lenses the people here call 'spectacles'

so I can see the little grey chips gleam

I tap my foot

line line line

dot dot dot

it is time to begin

on every dot, I pivot

for every line, I twirl

I dance into the heart of the storm

feeling the charge of lightning beneath my feet

alive and terrified at the same time

I develop a rhythm

and I repeat it

dancing the dance of the storm

I murmur a prayer to the Wandering God

asking for his guidance with my steps

but that, if I fail

I can see *him* again

and ask for forgiveness

for a while, it seems endless

dot dot

dance dance

line line

spin spin

I almost stop

thinking all my motions futile

as the little silver gleams control the storm without pause

then it all stops

there is no more lightning or thunder

only dark clouds and silver dust remain streaming through the

air

the particles look like little stars

glowing and gleaming in the darkness

the cells start to change their pattern

dot line dot

dot line

dot dot

line dot

is it a question?

all I can do is repeat the pattern

and hope

the silver dust moves on its own

becoming a silver cloudling

shrouding the sky in darkness

the clouds darken

pregnant and bursting

I feel the first drop hit me on the forehead

I look up

the sky, dark and desolate

cries its first tears

dripping

then drizzling

into rain

I do not know what was said

but the storm has changed

only distant rumblings of thunder remain now

the door is open

then I see *him*

the shock on *his* face fills me with joy

he is wrapped in rope and chains

unable to move

a leash around his neck

holding it is the dragon

with chains on his own wings

blank shock on his face

how?

had he been there, all this time

following us?

were we the ones being hunted all this time?

I realize that it doesn't matter

there is fear on his face now

we have found them at last

XV. Rescue

I don't wait

I lung at the hunter

the captor who had led us on this trip

my frustration grows in midair

he had led us on this merry chase

when all the while he'd been right here

but he isn't like other dragons

he isn't surprised by my anger

there is no fear of us

only disgust

distaste for my daring to swing at him

he moves aside

evading my clumsy lunge

not responding right away

his eyes show cunning

deviousness, danger

he is taking our measure

Will tries next, throwing punches

he grabs at the dragon's arm

trying to free our friend

but the dragon grabs Will

and tosses him

Nicki and I keep striking

punching

kicking

biting

doing whatever we can

he blocks

side-steps and parries our clumsy strikes

analyzing us

the dragon lets go of the chain

he topples to the ground, protesting

the dragon's disdain becomes a hideous grin

I do not like that face

he doesn't see us as people

but as animals to be put down

he thinks he is the predator here

the dragon lunges

launching his own thrusts and strikes now

I feel the hard swing of his fist

I fall to the ground

Nicki joins me

clutching her stomach

Will jumps on the dragon

riding it like a bull

grinning wildly

my old fears come back

watching the dragons had terrified me

they had owned me

used me

used us all

and they were going to try again

Will yells at me to dance

dance? Is he crazy?

I look to the silver cloudling in the sky

dance!

of course!

I still have the spectacles on

I start to move my feet

while Nicki and Will wrestle with the dragon

dot dot

dance dance

come on...

hurry...

I don't know how long they can hold him

the dragon seems to know what I am up to

his movements are faster

frantic

it is all Will and Nicki can do to hang on

I hustle

doing what I can to get the cloud's attention

suddenly, silence is all I hear

oh no

did he get them?

Nicki and Will lie still

the dragon looks over them, victorious

he looks at me

and I gulp

I'm next

I hear wild laughter

for a minute I am unnerved

then *he* arrives

jumping right on the hunter

his collar now only a chain

wrapping around the dragon's throat

he squeezes

how long had *he* been chained like that?

the raw hatred in *his* eyes

as he lives the nightmare of being a prisoner again

something I knew all too well while I was in that cell

I don't waste my chance

I dance

I twirl

mirroring the lines and dots

the cloud responds

changing its pattern again

dot dot dot

line

dot line dot

dot dot

line dot line

dot

I mirror the pattern

move for move

nearly completing the sequence

when I feel reptilian hands close in

and I am lifted into the air

all of them are down

it is just me and the dragon

there is fear in his eyes

he knows I have some way to talk to the storm

and he doesn't want me to make the lightning come again

so he is going to finish me

he raises his fist and I flinch

waiting for the pain to come

then I see *him* grab the dragon's chains

and pull

knocking the beast off balance

letting me go

I have to make this fast

I do the dance

faster than I thought possible

I move into the heart of the storm

and wait for the dragon to follow

finishing the last step as he grabs me and throws...

I hit the ground to the sound of thunder

but lightning hits the dragon

igniting him on fire

he hisses and screams in agony

as the lightning shocks and sears him

burning him from the inside out

he, too, would have his place with the bones

and so will I...

the lightning is starting again

I'm not sure I can make it back

I will never have the chance to dance again

but I am content

he is alive

they are alive

I have no problem

becoming one with the storm

then *he* runs in

chancing the lightning and the thunder

to grab my hand and pull me from the storm

that fool!

stupid, stupid idiot

why?

looking into his eyes

I know

XVI. Rain

the others are still alive

he'd wanted to capture us

not kill us

for whom and why, we do not know

Will has a bump on his head

Nicki has her own scars

but that still doesn't stop her from chiding him for his

foolishness

he shrugs it off
but I see him blush
and know he'd do it again

that is a concern for another day
today, I look at *him*
and *he* looks back at me
both of us trying to say something
yet, we can't

not every storm has abated
we had done things to each other
I had hated *him*
he had destroyed my life

part of me is furious
part of me might always be this angry
but I understand
after walking my own journey
I see now what *he* saw

no, I don't hate *him* anymore
in truth, I was scared
I thought I had lost *him*

after all we had been through

all the tears I held back because...

in finding *him*

I discovered myself

I no longer hate *him*

but having held on to my own storm for so long

I can't let it go

we look at each other

pain in each of our eyes

each mouthing that single solitary word

"sorry"

it is the key that opens the door

the tears come

the rain falls

I am finally able to let it all go

we hug

gripping each other tight

I feel trickles of tears run down *his* face

we had hurt each other

but no more

Will, Nicki, *the Watcher* and I

we are family

and our journey is only just beginning

tomorrow we will go

see what lurks beyond this storm

what worlds other than these dwell there

but today, we have each other

and it is enough

About the Creative Team

Joshua Pantalleresco writes stuff. It's even on his business card. This is a succinct way of saying that in addition to writing poetry, he also does interviews, columns, comics, prose and anything possible with the written word. When he isn't writing, he's playing with podcasts, filming stuff, fiddling with alternative medicine, travelling, talking to people and pretending he is a rockstar. When he isn't attempting to be artistic, he tries to foil his villainous rivals John Tinkess, Diana Bonaventure and The Chaos Ewok in Words with Friends with mixed results (but at least he almost always crushes his sister.)

Stormdancer is his second book through Mirror World Publishing. He lives in Calgary. His webpage is http://jpantalleresco.wordpress.com and his twitter is @jpantalleresco.

Florence Chan is an illustrator, designer and 3D modeller from Calgary, Alberta, now living in Toronto, Canada. She is the illustrator of Marilyn Marsh Noll's 'Jonathan and the Magical Broomstick' and Joshua Pantalleresco's 'The Watcher' and has contributed to Jason Mehmel's comic anthology 'Fight Comics' as well as Damian Willcox's 'Dorkboy: 1995-2015 Two Dorkades and Counting'.

Her work can be found at www.florencechan.ca

Kristen Denbow is always on the lookout for interesting projects and ideas to pursue. She enjoys working with others collaboratively and creatively to help accomplish this. The Watcher series is one that is dear to her heart. Finding the creative aspect of anything she does is her passion. She also edits, designs and writes, whenever, whatever and however she can. In her spare time she contemplates the universe, reads about psychology and dabbles in cosplay, her favorite genre being Steampunk.

M|W mirror world publishing

To learn more about our authors and our current projects visit:
www.mirrorworldpublishing.com, follow @MirrorWorldPub or like us at
www.facebook.com/mirrorworldpublishing

*We appreciate every like, tweet, facebook post and review and we love to hear from
you. Please consider leaving us a review online or sending your thoughts and comments
to info@mirrorworldpublishing.com*

Thank you.

CPSIA information can be obtained at www.ICGtesting.com
Printed in the USA
LVOW11s2331120816

500141LV00001B/17/P

9 780994 749031